First published 2006 by Walker Books Ltd
87 Vauxhall Walk, London SE11 5HJ

2 4 6 8 10 9 7 5 3 1

Text and Illustrations © 2006 Ted Sieger
The author/illustrator has asserted his moral rights.

Inspired by *The Story of the Other Wise Man* by Henry van Dyke

This book has been typeset in Gararond and Fontesque

Printed in China

British Library Cataloguing in Publication Data:
a catalogue record for this book is
available from the British Library

ISBN-10: 0-7445-7009-3
ISBN-13: 978-0-7445-7009-0

www.walkerbooks.co.uk

THE FOURTH KING

WALKER BOOKS
AND SUBSIDIARIES
LONDON · BOSTON · SYDNEY · AUCKLAND

TED SIEGER

ONCE UPON A TIME, THREE KINGS CAME OUT OF A DISTANT LAND and followed a star to a little town across the desert. You may know them as the Wise Men, or the Magi, or, as I did, by their names: Melchior, Caspar and Balthazar. They brought with them gold, frankincense and myrrh, presents for a newborn child.

But there was another king who set out on the long and difficult journey. Unlike the others, he arrived too late and empty-handed. I was that king ... King Mazzel. I was the Fourth King.

I WAS THE RULER of a very small kingdom. So small that I was its king and its people! Indeed, if it had not been for my camel, Chamberlin, I would have been all alone — alone except for the stars, my distant friends.

Like the Three Kings, I was a stargazer. Night after night I scoured the sky for the sign that would herald the birth of the King of Kings. Night after night I searched in vain. How long had I watched? A thousand nights? Ten thousand?

A<small>ND</small> <small>THEN</small>, that long-awaited night, it happened — the sign, appearing after all these years!

My heart skipped a beat with joy: in an instant we ran out the door ... only to run back in again.

After all, a king had been born — we couldn't show up without a present! I put on my royal cloak and packed my most valuable possessions: the royal star map and the royal star crystal.

We were on our way.

WE HAD TO HURRY: the Three Kings
were waiting at the edge of the great
desert and the four of us would
continue our journey together.

We rode through the night, leaving our home far behind, but I felt safe with the star as my guide. The desert plain drew nearer, and I looked forward to seeing my friends. But then the breeze freshened and stung our eyes with dust; the wind howled and bellowed; and the sandstorm started...

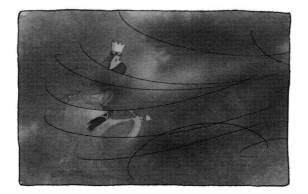

AFRAID FOR OUR LIVES, we ploughed on through wave after wave of sand, hoping to outrun the storm and find shelter — but it seemed hopeless. And then, just as we were ready to drop in the dunes, we staggered out of the storm and into stillness.

It was Chamberlin who heard it first — a small cry on the wind. What were we to do? My friends waiting; our journey, and such a long journey, still ahead of us. What were we to do?

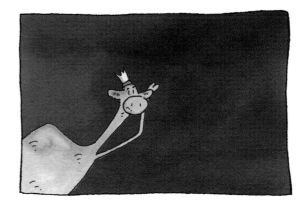

We headed back into the storm, and there, in its heart, we found a little nomad girl — sand-stung and frightened, her name blown away by the wind.

I wrapped her in my cloak and carried her through the blizzard.

We were glad to have found her and glad, too, when her family found us. They invited us to stay, but I was anxious to join my friends.

We rode on, confident that we could make up the time. Yet when we arrived, the Three Kings had already left. We had missed them by minutes!

"MY DEAR MAZZEL," said the note. "We waited as long as we could; we have set off across the desert. One travels faster than three, and we are certain to see you before the journey's end. Your friend, Balthazar."

They weren't far ahead; we would surely catch up!

Chamberlin galloped faster than he had ever galloped in his life. But Chamberlin was quite a bit smaller than most camels, and his legs, though strong, weren't quite as long!

At last, I spied them in the distance...

ONLY IT WASN'T THEM, it was a merchant caravan —

we weren't the only ones travelling that night. The merchants

were lost and without a map — could I help them, perhaps?

But such a long camel train would travel very slowly. What were

we to do? My heart sank: we were already late — what were we to do?

So, we followed my star map: it was quite a detour to their hometown.

In slow procession, we led the caravan safely out of the desert. My heart soared:

I could still see the star; perhaps we would meet up with the Three Kings after all…

BUT THEN a deep gorge cut across our path.
There was no way round it; we would have
to cross over! The merchants were scared;
their camels were scared; I was scared!
  But Chamberlin was with me,
and his courage
inspired us all...

How we all made it, I will never know ...

...but we did!

WE TRAVELLED ON, following the star into the mountains.

The road grew steeper now, the wind grew icy, and the raindrops

turned to hailstones. It was cold and our steps were shivery, but

Chamberlin didn't seem to mind. I held on tightly to him, afraid

we would lose sight of each other.

A small plant looked up at us, withered and thirsty. I gave it what little water we had left.

To our amazement, the plant began to flower, then dropped into my palm a little, round fruit that sounded like a bell.

We were astonished, and not a little puzzled; but the star was calling and I was anxious to join our friends, and so...

AT THE OUTSKIRTS OF THEIR TOWN, we bade farewell to the merchants.
So they wouldn't get lost again, we left the royal star map with the merchants and then set off.

The night was cool and silent and the star glimmered like a candle in a faraway window.
We rode until we were weary, and then stopped in need of rest.

It was Chamberlin who heard it first — a tiny, tinkling bell on the breeze. We looked around,
but there was no one there — what were we to do? The tinkling came again...

Finally we climbed above the clouds and found ourselves at the very top of the mountain.

The star burned brightly and, full of hope once more, we tumbled after our friends.

OUR DESCENT WAS RAPID,
and I felt sure we would catch
the Three Kings very soon.
But now we found our path blocked
by a strange, endless wall that bore
no gates or doorways.

There was no way through it;
we would have to go round it.
We hurried by as quickly as we could,
unsure of what was on the other side.

We were almost past its boundary
when we discovered the
terrible truth...

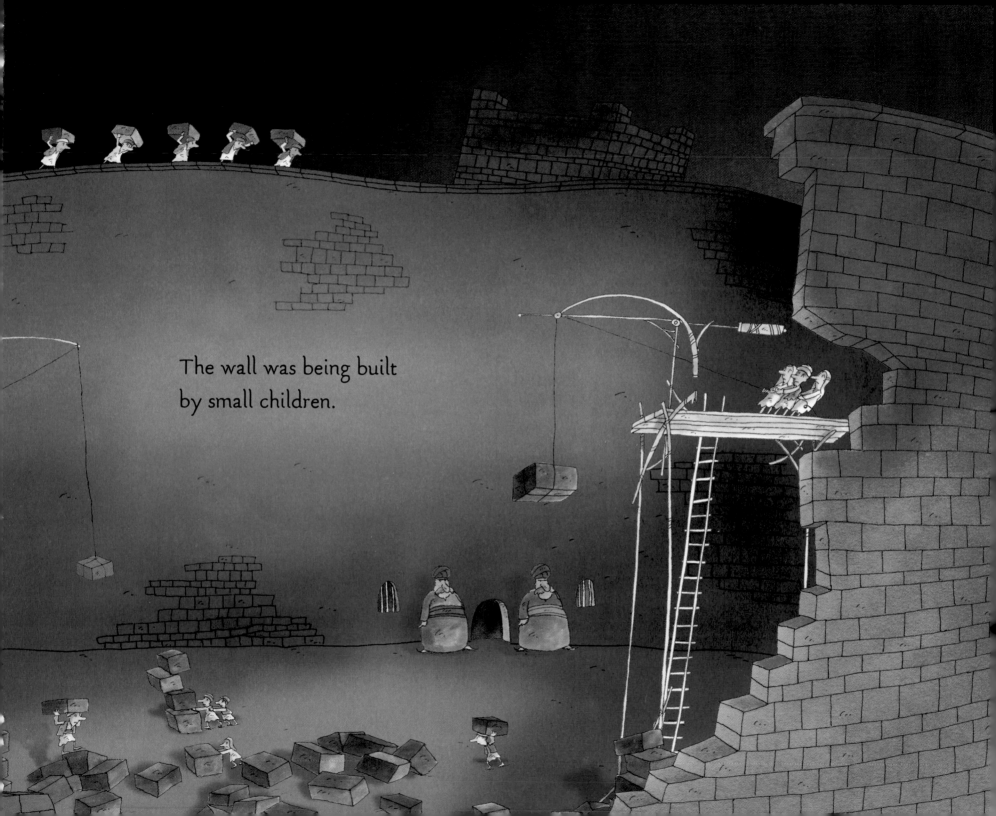

The wall was being built
by small children.

THE CHILDREN WERE SLAVES belonging to a rich man who forced them to work on his wall. His guards seized us and carried us inside. I commanded the rich man to let the children go, but he just laughed.

I offered to give up my last gift for the newborn king in exchange for the children's freedom. The rich man snatched the crystal and said that it was ransom enough for my camel and me, that we were free to go — but no one else.

What were we to do?

AND SO, we stayed with the children — and toiled with them to finish the wall. As we laboured, so the stones piled higher and hid the star from our view. And in spite of Chamberlin's best efforts to keep me from despair, my hopes were fading fast.

Seeing my sadness, a little girl gave me her only possession — a toy lamb carved from wood. It made me smile. I hid the lamb in my tunic and promised her that, somehow, we would all be free...

BUT NOT YET. Instead, we were herded into a dark, stone maze. We could hardly see each other in the blackness, but the children huddled close to me and Chamberlin. Outside, the guards slept. This was our chance ... if only we could see to escape.

It was Chamberlin who heard it first — a tiny, tinkling bell in the silence: the fruit from the desert.

It cracked open in my hand to reveal three softly luminous star-seeds — and their light shone in the darkness. Chamberlin led us on tiptoes, past the sleeping guards and out of our prison. We lifted the children through the last small opening in the wall — we were free!

THE CHILDREN CAME WITH US. I felt sure they would be safe with the newborn king. The star called us on towards a little town – Bethlehem.

There we met some shepherds with glad tidings. They had followed the star to a stable; they had visited a baby and seen the Three Kings. My heart sang with joy!

But the shepherds stopped us. Something terrible was happening in Bethlehem: soldiers sent to kill the King of Kings were killing children.

That tiny baby born in a stable – I had to save him!

WE LEFT THE CHILDREN WITH THE SHEPHERDS and raced down the hillside. But soldiers were searching the valley, so we hid amongst the ruins and waited for them to go. Then out of the shadows, a man appeared leading a donkey carrying a woman with a baby in her arms. They looked frightened, and the infant was starting to stir, so I beckoned them to our hiding place — not a moment too soon.

How silently we sat as the soldiers passed by — except for the newborn child, who started to whimper. Quickly, I gave him the wooden lamb from my pocket, and he beamed with hushed delight.

   But the soldiers had turned back and were coming closer. What were we to do? They were sure to discover us — what were we to do?

IN THE END there was only one thing to do. With a deep breath, I leapt out onto the road, Chamberlin at my side, and ran, hoping that we could distract the soldiers long enough for the family to make their escape.

Sure enough, the soldiers gave chase and were soon gaining on us; but somehow we drew our pursuers into the next valley, before I stumbled to a stop, exhausted. Chamberlin stood guard as the troops closed in, their swords drawn menacingly. We were outnumbered and, it seemed, out of luck…

To this day, I don't know what happened next; but certainly the earth shook and our ears were full of thunder. And the soldiers? They were much afraid and fled in confusion. I cannot be certain, but I like to think that they had been scattered by the trampling of three royal camels...

Chamberlin and I were alone on the edge of town. The stable that the shepherds had spoken about was up ahead — we ran, we ran as fast as we could ... but the stable was empty. We were too late! Our journey had been in vain. I fell to my knees and wept.

AND THEN, IN THE DEPTHS
OF MY DESPAIR, the most wonderful
thing happened: I heard a voice
speak softly…

"King Mazzel, you have not come too late!
You were always with me.
When I was lost, you showed me the way.
When I was thirsty, you gave me water.
When I was captive, you freed me.
When I was in danger, you saved me.
You were always there
when I needed you,
and I will be with you for ever."

HEARING THESE WORDS, I knew that my journey was over. My heart was filled with joy. The rising sun felt warm on my face. A new day was dawning.

Outside the stable, the shepherds and the children were waiting. Full of smiles, we embraced and set off for their farmlands and new pastures.

AND SO, though it hardly matters now, I never did meet the Three Kings.
Balthazar, Caspar and Melchior returned to their kingdoms, but I did not.

I am no longer a king: I am a shepherd, and Chamberlin is a sheep-camel.
He looks after our sheep, and I look after our flock of children. We are very happy.

From time to time we still like to walk in the meadow and watch the night sky.
And though the star has long disappeared from its place,
it still burns brightly in my heart.